PENICILLIN

Kenny Abdo

An Imprint of Abdo Zoom
abdobooks.com

abdobooks.com

Published by Abdo Zoom, a division of ABDO, P.O. Box 398166, Minneapolis, Minnesota 55439. Copyright © 2024 by Abdo Consulting Group, Inc. International copyrights reserved in all countries. No part of this book may be reproduced in any form without written permission from the publisher. Fly!™ is a trademark and logo of Abdo Zoom.

Printed in the United States of America, North Mankato, Minnesota.
102023
012024

Photo Credits: Alamy, Bridgeman Images, Getty Images, Granger Collection, Shutterstock
Production Contributors: Kenny Abdo, Jennie Forsberg, Grace Hansen
Design Contributors: Candice Keimig, Neil Klinepier, Colleen McLaren

Library of Congress Control Number: 2023938001

Publisher's Cataloging-in-Publication Data

Names: Abdo, Kenny, author.
Title: Penicillin / by Kenny Abdo
Description: Minneapolis, Minnesota : Abdo Zoom, 2024 | Series: Accidental science discoveries | Includes online resources and index.
Identifiers: ISBN 9781098284121 (lib. bdg.) | ISBN 9781098284848 (eBook) | ISBN 9781098285203 (Read-to-Me eBook)
Subjects: LCSH: Penicillin--Juvenile literature. | Antibiotics--Juvenile literature. | Serendipity in science--Juvenile literature. | Inventions--Juvenile literature. | Discoveries in science--Juvenile literature.
Classification: DDC 500--dc23

TABLE OF CONTENTS

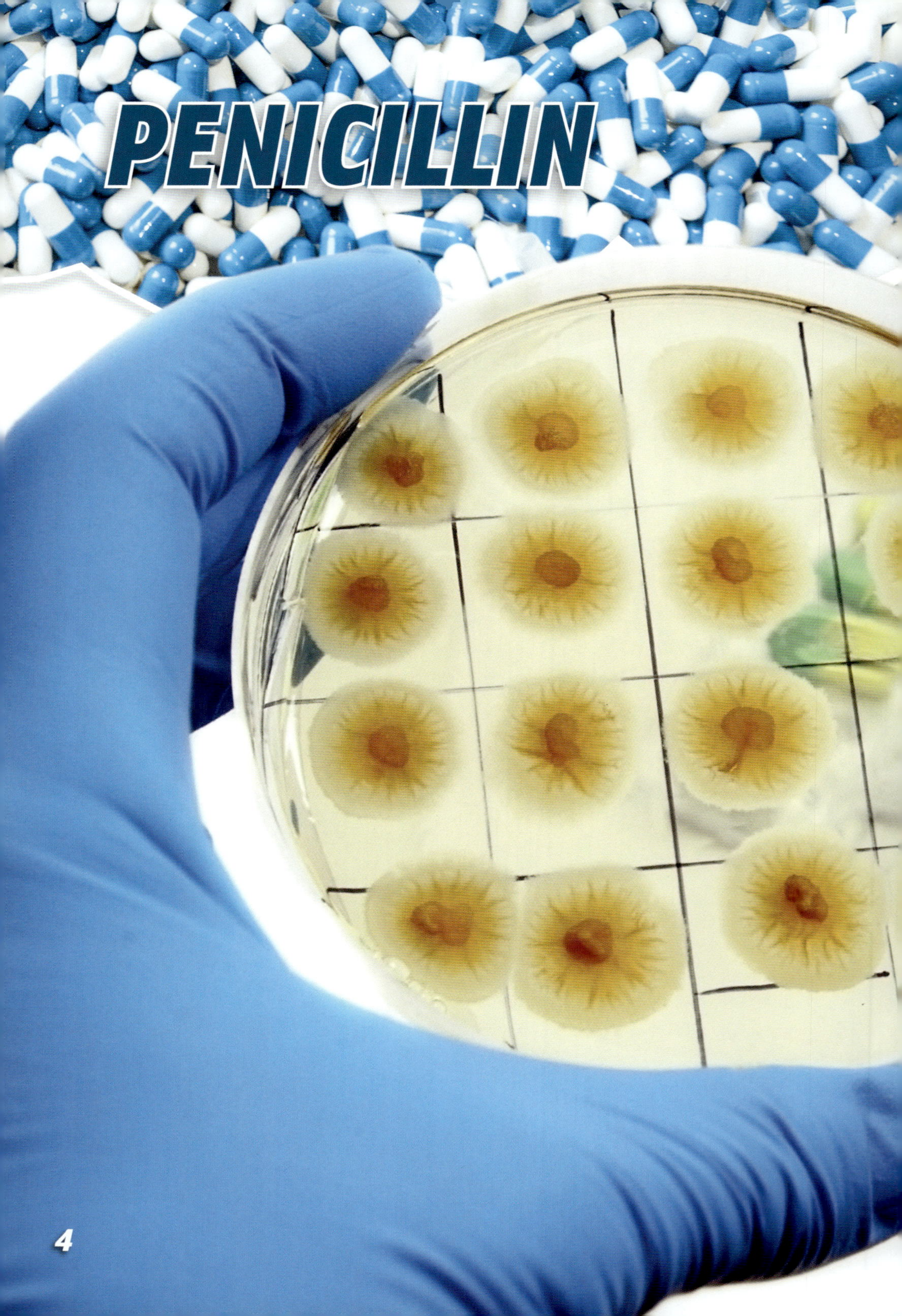

PENICILLIN

With the accidental discovery of penicillin, not only were countless lives saved, but a new era in medicine had begun!

THE ACCIDENT

In 1928, Scottish **microbiologist** Alexander Fleming left a **Petri dish** of bacteria in his laboratory while on vacation. When he returned, he found mold growing in the Petri dish.

The mold was preventing the bacteria from growing. Fleming realized that the mold produced a self-defense chemical that could kill bacteria. He named the substance penicillin.

Fleming published his discoveries and presented his work to the **Medical Research Club**. Unfortunately, his peers showed little interest in his work. Fleming gave up shortly after that.

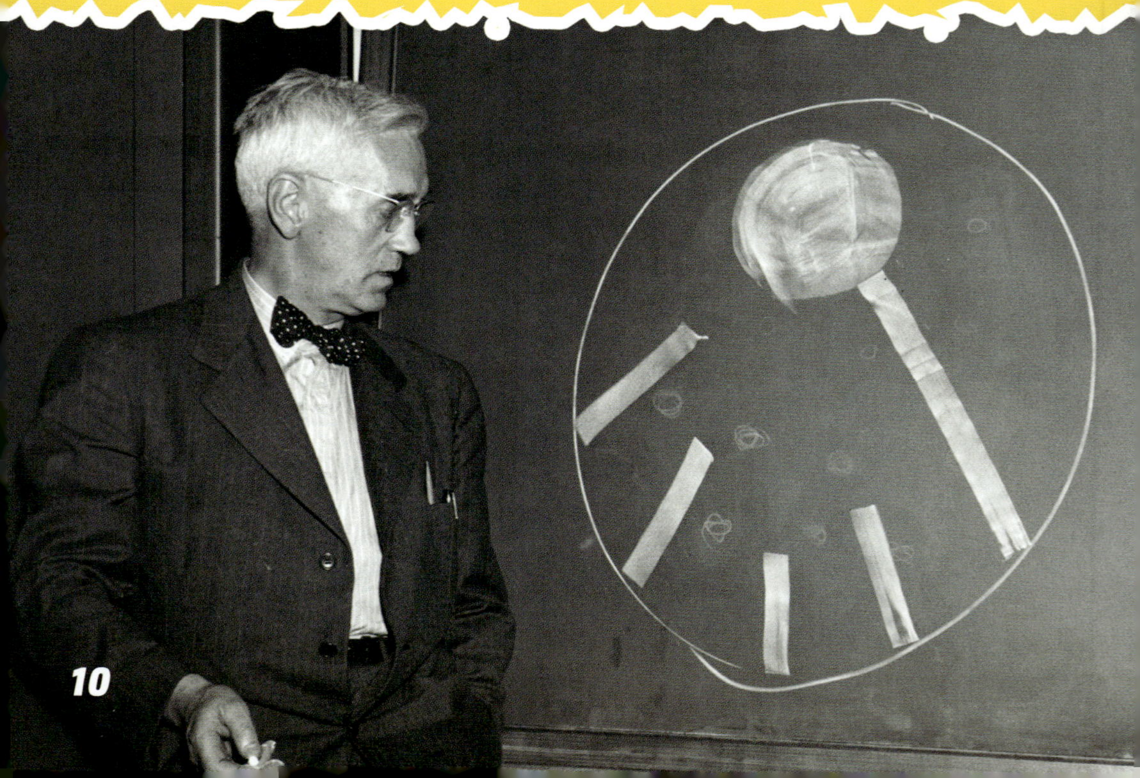

Ernst Chain

In 1937, scientists Howard Florey and
Ernst Chain found Fleming's study.
With their own team, they began
work on the Penicillin Project. However,
US drug companies were not very
helpful.

Howard Florey

Thanks to PENICILLIN
...He Will Come Home!

That all changed during **World War II**. Penicillin helped treat infections and saved soldiers' lives. In 1945, Florey and Chain won the **Nobel Prize** in Medicine. They shared the award with Fleming.

SERVEL
PENICILLIN
50 BOTTLES 100,000 OXFORD UNITS EACH
STORE AT TEMPERATURE OF LESS THAN 10° CENT.
EXPIRES
CHAS. PFIZER & CO., Inc., N.Y., N.Y.

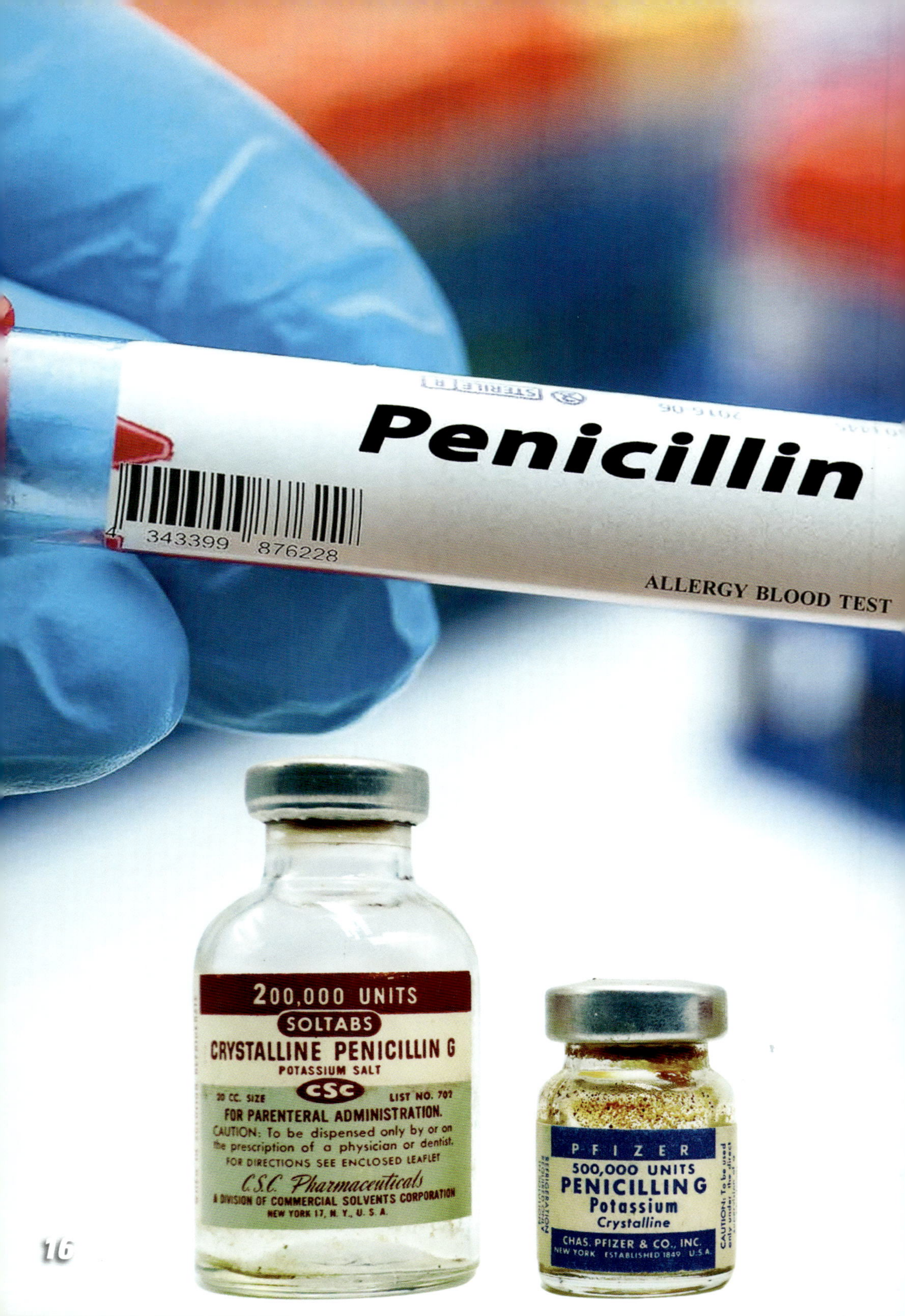
Penicillin
STERILE R
2016.06
ALLERGY BLOOD TEST
200,000 UNITS
SOLTABS
CRYSTALLINE PENICILLIN G
POTASSIUM SALT
CSC
20 CC. SIZE
LIST NO. 702
FOR PARENTERAL ADMINISTRATION.
CAUTION: To be dispensed only by or on
the prescription of a physician or dentist.
FOR DIRECTIONS SEE ENCLOSED LEAFLET
C.S.C. Pharmaceuticals
A DIVISION OF COMMERCIAL SOLVENTS CORPORATION
NEW YORK 17, N. Y., U. S. A.
PFIZER
500,000 UNITS
PENICILLIN G
Potassium
Crystalline
CHAS. PFIZER & CO., INC.
NEW YORK   ESTABLISHED 1849   U.S.A.

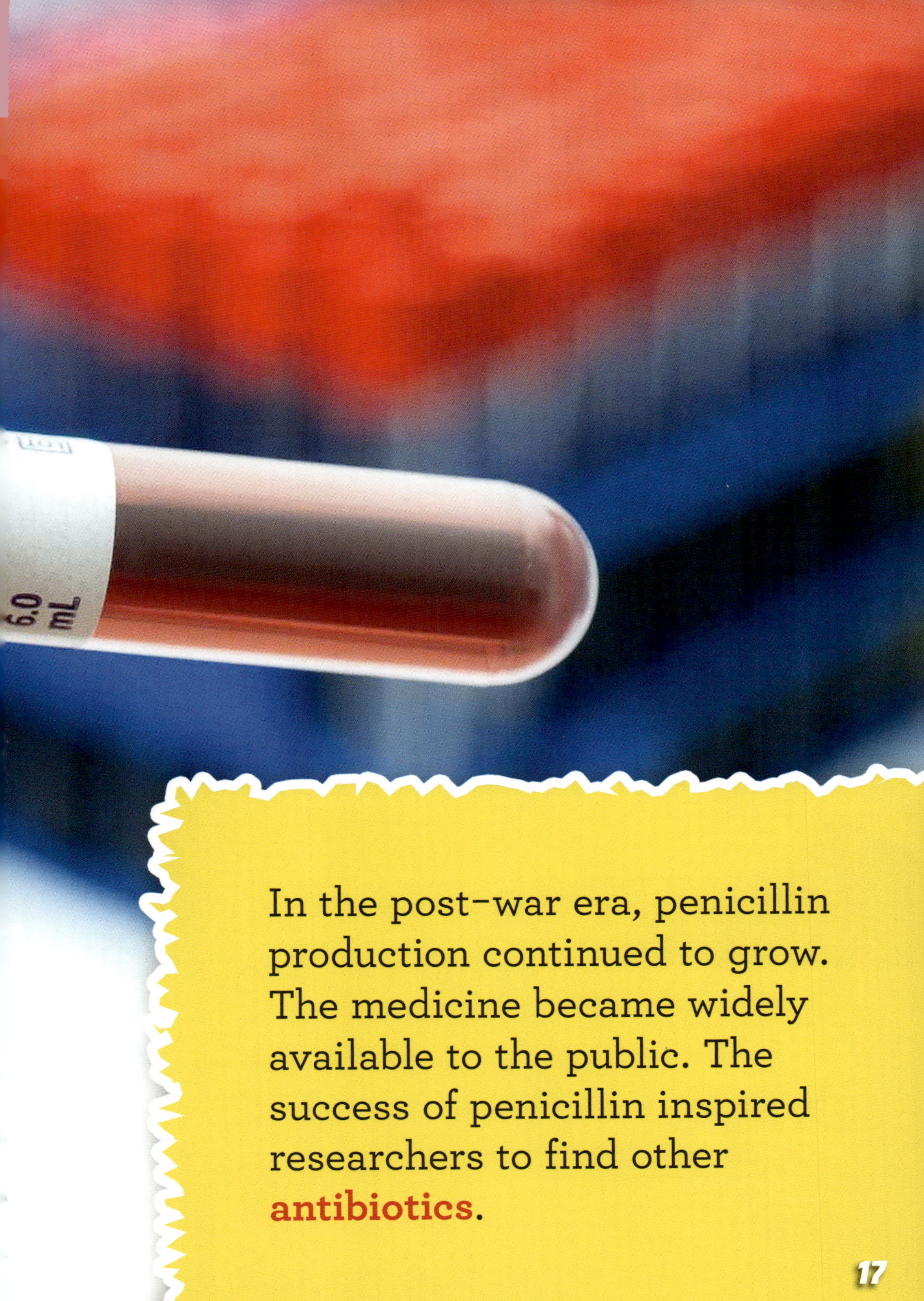

In the post-war era, penicillin production continued to grow. The medicine became widely available to the public. The success of penicillin inspired researchers to find other **antibiotics**.

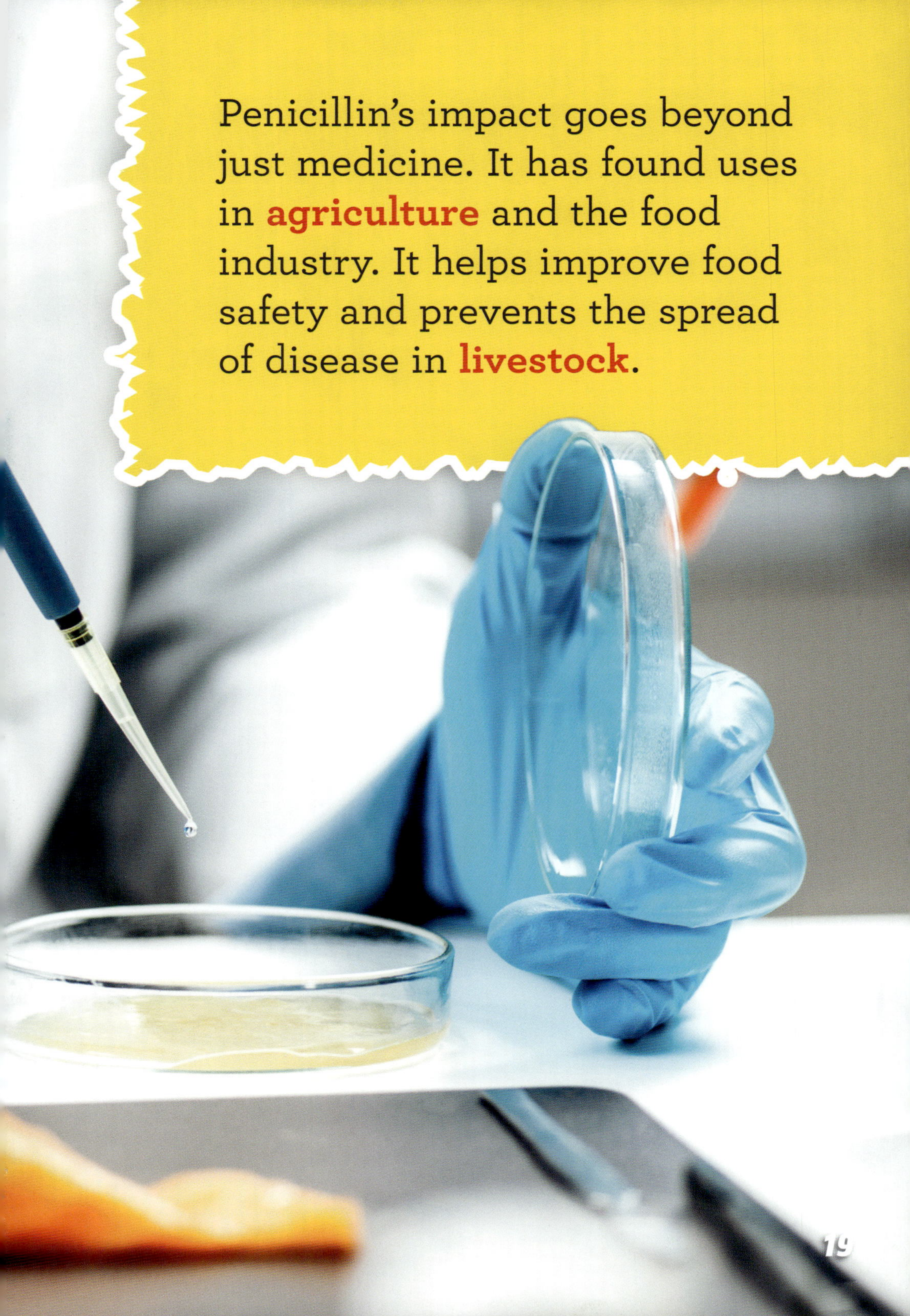

Penicillin's impact goes beyond just medicine. It has found uses in **agriculture** and the food industry. It helps improve food safety and prevents the spread of disease in **livestock**.

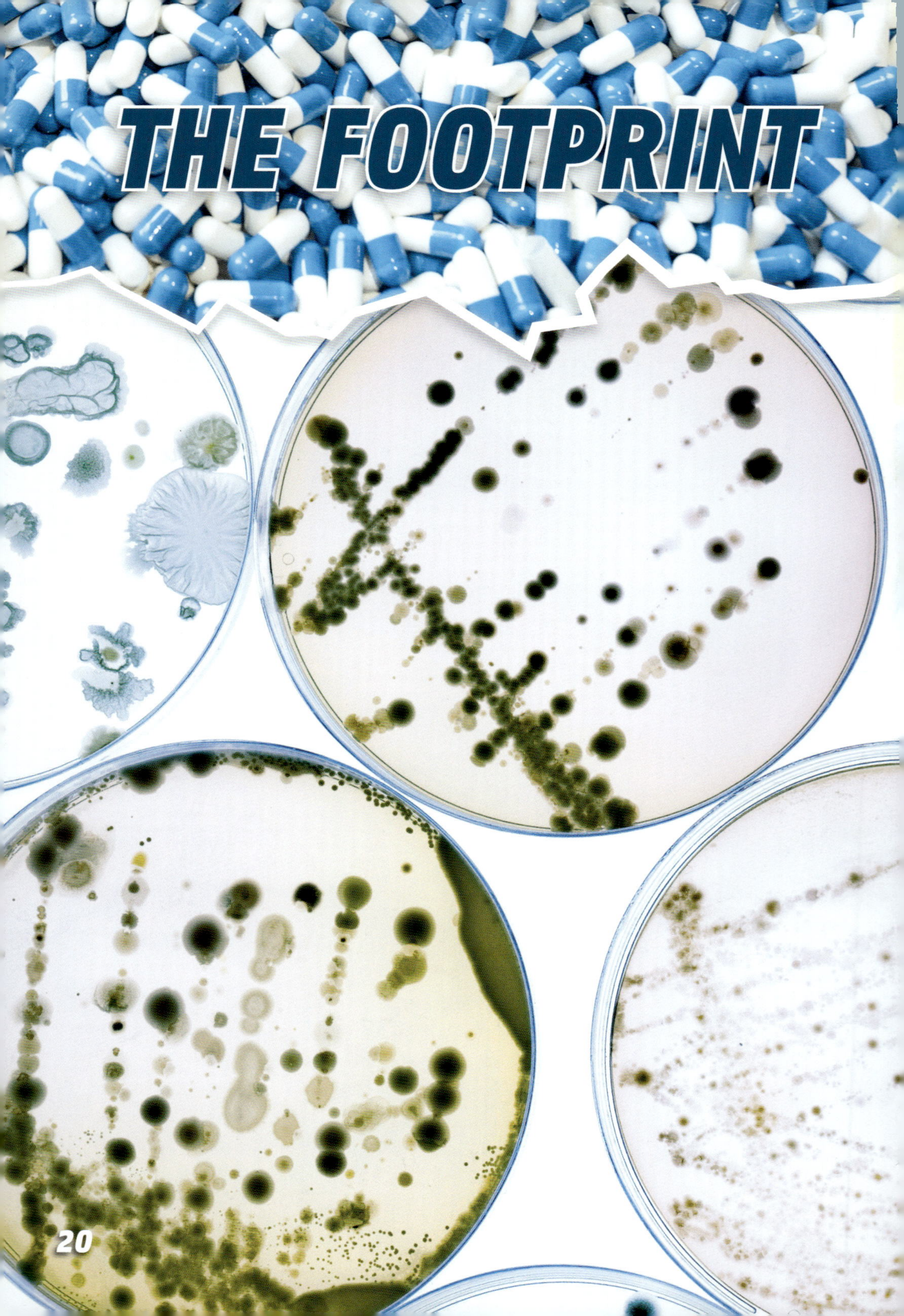

THE FOOTPRINT
20

Today, penicillin remains a key piece in the advancement of modern medicine. With scientists discovering new ways to fight infection, there is a lot more room to grow!

GLOSSARY

agriculture – the science of farming, including the growing of crops and the caring of animals to provide food.

antibiotic – a substance used to kill germs that cause disease.

livestock – animals that are kept and raised on a farm to provide goods like meat, milk, and eggs.

Medical Research Club – founded in 1891, it is a group of scientists and doctors who research and experiment with medicinal discoveries.

microbiologist – a scientist who studies microscopic life forms such as bacteria, algae, and fungi.

Nobel Prize – international awards given to those who have achieved the "greatest benefit to humankind" that year.

Petri dish – a small round dish of thin glass or plastic used for growing organisms like cells, bacteria, or fungus.

World War II – (1939–1945) a war fought in Europe, Asia, and Africa. Great Britain, France, the United States, the Soviet Union, and their allies were on one side. Germany, Italy, Japan, and their allies were on the other side.

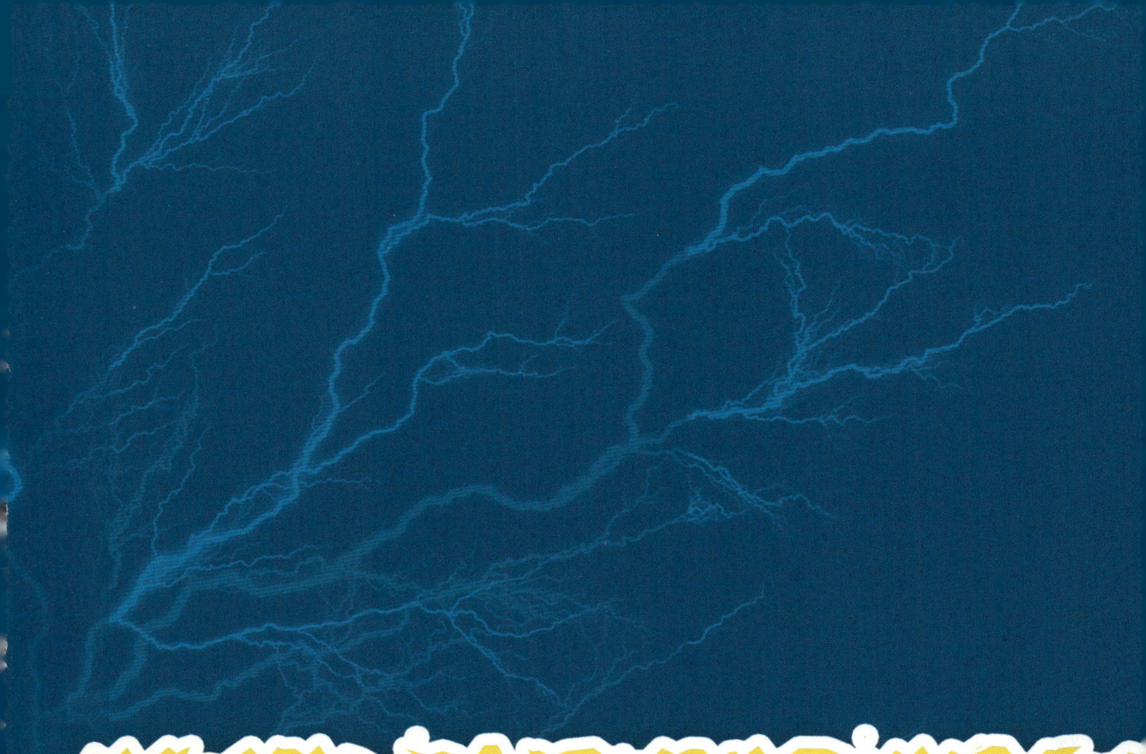

ONLINE RESOURCES

To learn more about penicillin, please visit **abdobooklinks.com** or scan this QR code. These links are routinely monitored and updated to provide the most current information available.

INDEX